How the Chrysanthemums Came to Have Their Colors

and other stories and poems

Yale Ryan Kwon

A GAMER'S TRIUMPH: FROM TRIUMPH TO DESPAIR

We are great buddies

Real fun to hang out with

Cool games to play on

We are free for now

Leaving work for vacation

School is out for now

We work together

Lurking in our rooms gaming

Late into the night

We are looted now

Striking foes using blitzkrieg

Straight to victory

We celebrate now

Singing in joy of our win

Sinning by stealing

We travel farther

The Thinning pathways thrill us

Grinning till it hurts

We get too prideful

Jazzing with the sounds of gain

June's heat distracts us

We move one too far

Falling into the abyss

Soon we will rage quit

TABLE OF CONTENTS

POEMS

WHERE WILL WE GO?

Bombs and bullets throughout Eastern Europe

For nearly two years:

Millions forced out of their homes,

Forced to see home for the first time – ruins.

The land – diseased with mines,

The Earth's skin – inflamed,

Bugs' buzz biting her to satisfy their unending hunger.

Dragons tear into her flesh,

Indent her face,

Bombard her with headaches.

There seems to be no end to her illness.

And we? We are the children whom she has adopted,

Yet we are the cause of her sickness:

We have set off bombs and bullets,

We have covered her in mines,

We have razed cities to the ground,

We have lured the buzzing to her,

We have engraved these dragons'-teeth trenches into her flesh.

Will we continue?

The Earth suffers, too hospitable to our torture,

And we do nothing to help?

Over what are we fighting?

If only death and destruction remain,

What value do we find in our feuds?

Enough!

Listen:

The Earth needs quiet.

She longs for peace,

She longs for happiness.

Outside of the scorching light of those who wrestle,

Of those who are starved by greed,

There are those who mourn in the shadows,

Who see the suffering, pain, and blight.

They are the ones who help the Earth,

They are the ones who see our mistakes,

They are the ones who listen

When the Earth cries softly:

Where will you go?

Where will you go when I am gone?

WE'VE GOT YOU COVERED

Our school isn't known for sports

In fact, we're known for our bad sports records

But the swim team's a different story

Surprisingly, we're the best in our district

And I'm proud to be part of the team

The people are all so unique

There are the goofy people,

The serious people,

The weird and sort of normal people,

They're all really good at swimming

Because it's our swim team,

Not all of us swim though

Obviously, there are the coaches

But

There's also us—

The managers

The coaches want a spreadsheet?

The Gold Moose Talent

Give us 20 minutes

What was your time last meet?

We've got you covered

Worried you'll miss an event during a meet?

Never worry

We're the ultimate team

A well-oiled machine

Run by elite brains

You'll always know where to find us

Is it practice?

5 feet from the pool, we have our criss-cross applesauce circle

Computers out, shoes off

Is it a meet?

Don't doubt us

We'll be timing our team, sharing snacks, and drinking Coke

I'll be in my red foldable chair protected by my towel

Why the towel?

You'd be surprised by the 4 feet waves people make when they flip-turn

Are we not timing?

(I'm not slacking, I promise. I just went to the vending machines)

You'll find us handing out event cards

We'll make sure no one skips

Us managers

We're the cool kids in this group

But we're still one big family
A chaotic one

QUARANTINE

2020 was the start of a new decade

It meant starting over

But the world had other plans for us

Corona 19—painful—deadly

Hit us all hard in the gut

Drastic changes

Staying at home almost all of the time

Going out with stuffy masks

TP short on stock

The internet rises

The stock market falls

We will survive at home

Online all the time

25/7

THE MIRACLE

All day it's work, work, work

Morning school, afternoon homework

Staring at a screen all day

My restless body aching to run

Nothing can save me from this misery

The only break is food

Sustaining me to finish my work

Suddenly I hear the sound of the doorbell

The greetings and talking

I know someone is there but who?

Then the ring of the familiar voice

A friend, buddy, my partner in crime

I am free from work

I can rest

And hang out with my friend

It is a miracle

TIME TRAVEL

There are so many times

When I want to journey through time

To correct my mistakes

That are regrets like a snake

Lurking in my mind all the time

I wish I could travel through time

To reverse the wrongs of my life

To learn from the mistakes of our forefathers

And experience the rights of the past

To open my eyes

And to see the world

In a way I have not seen before

I may not be able to meddle

But I will learn from the pain of the people

To fix my wrongs of the past

How I would like to travel through time

To see the fate of my actions

Before they become present

So I may find the best course of action

To be as happy as can be

Oh, how I'd like to travel through time
To observe the events of time

THE BOMB

Like every day

I wake up

Worried that I am no more because

Hades has claimed my life

During the fighting

Many lives were sacrificed

I do not wish mine to join them

The commotion outside

Is peculiar

The air is out of place

In this cozy town I live in

My gut tells me to face my fears once more

I stumble outside

A shadow on my face

That is not a cloud

Loud buzzing, nullifying all the noise

Only when I hear the whistling

Do I realize

And lookup

To see my fate

It's too late, my brain tells me

The voices echo throughout my head and say

Give up just like all the other times

But in an instant, it all changes

The bad voices disappear, replaced with new ones

Maybe I can get away, they say

Maybe I can survive

Maybe it's not too late

As my legs start accelerating

I look back into the sky

And see that I still have time

Or do I…

The good voices I have are soon drowned out

By evil cries telling me to stop and accept my fate

Unknowingly my legs have slowed to a stop

And when I stand still, I hear the sound of the blast

Am I far away enough?

SOLITUDE / PRIDE / TRANQUILITY

I. Solitude

So there's this thing

where I know everybody's footsteps

I know my mom and dad's footsteps

I know my sister's footsteps

I know my dog's

and I know my grandma's

Somedays the lack of footsteps tells me I'm home alone

And there's no one there to tell me what to do

I sleep in

I need to sleep

I like to sleep

If I'm hungry I make my own food

because that's also fun

No one's there to nag me

or tell me I'm doing something wrong

It can get silent after a while

but you get used to it

II. Pride

I took notice of it

as I would

because it's very loud.

I was hoping

to catch it

when it was staying still

(you know how flies will land on the wall sometimes)

but it got close to me

one too many times

and by instinct

I BAM

I thwacked it

and it dropped dead

and I was proud.

III. Tranquility

Whenever I'm up

Early in the morning

It always feels

So

Peaceful

When I go outside

I put on my slippers

And just wander around

I'm just thinking

About

Whatever pops into my head first

It seems to me

That the trees around me

Are all so

Still

It feels as if

They're sitting down on the ground

Staring into the distance

Watching the pastel sky

And pink clouds floating about

With the morning dew glazing the plants

When I walk on the grass

The morning dew soaks into my shoes

Refreshing me

There are no bugs

No mosquitoes

No gnats

And no flies

To disturb my thinking

At some moment in time

The sunlight wakes up

Changing from its pastel skies

To the cheerful yellow we all know

At some point in time

The light awakens the world

In that bright yellow

When I finally realize that

The pastel skies are gone

I go back inside

Because

The morning dew vanishes

And the bugs

The mosquitoes

The gnats

And the flies

They all come back

All those thoughts

My peaceful thinking

My walk

They all flutter away

And so I wait

For another day

When the pastel skies are back

And I wait

For another day

When I'm not too lazy

When I'm not too busy sleeping in

MY TJ LIFE

TJ,

Oh, so much had I heard,

Both good and bad,

I hoped the truth was good

Now as a Colonial,

I can testify,

The journey that I've took

Oh, festivals galore!

We've celebrated the Chinese New years

With games, food, and performances

Like dancing fireflies

Of Latin and swim,

I've traveled to convention and districts

To see my peers and I, reach new heights

But not everything can be perfect

In this place called school

I've through vectors, Krebs, and CS

Competed with top-tier brains

But now it's the final stretch of freshman year

Full of projects and finals

It's like no other year I've trekked through

But I'll endure it all,

And end this year's journey victorious

To prepare for 3 years

In this TJ life, I will have

Thou who hast invited and nurtured young minds, Many have strived to enter thy domain, But only a select few got the invitation, And the guests arrive with much expectation.

Upon entering, I've learned time management, And Biology has become my favorite companion, Lab reports and papers await us each week, And we greet them with zeal and passion.

Vector, Krebs Cycle, and Shakespeare, We have encountered them with glee, Into the night, Time take flight,

And the light breaks through the night.

Latin Convention and Swim Meet

A welcome exercise for our mind and body, Many have been willing participants,

Hoping to please thee with our talents.

When we leave and enter the world,

When old age shall claim us all,

Thou shalt remain bestowing Beauty and Truth, To all those who enter thy domain.

A YEAR IN ISOLATION: FROM DARKNESS TO LIGHT

You came into my life very suddenly.

It was the start of a new year and decade

Starting anew with resolutions

When you struck quicker than lightning

Many fell sick

The world locked down into a panic

And I grew distant with the world,

Only being able to contact close friends.

For one year I stood stuck in the safety of my home

Looking at a rectangle of light

When two piercing needles granted me permission

To explore the world again

THE OCEAN OF LIFE

When you sail the vast ocean,

What do you see?

On the calm ocean-blue

All I see is blue, blue, and blue

Would you like some blue?

The gentle waves rocking your boat like a crib

The sun's warm rays comfort you

Where are you sailing?

When you sail the ocean,

But the world's a storm,

What will you do?

The waves rise above you

Attempting to swallow you

The thunder ringing in your ears

Clouds staining the blue sky

Rain battering against the deck

Where will you go?

When the storm takes you off course

And the sun peaks open

Your vessel in shambles

Sails in shreds

Hull with holes

Water leaking through

How will you find your way back?

Maybe by chance

If you trust the current

You might just find a way

Or maybe through expertise

But you'll be fine

Although it's hard to see

The way of the world has a path for you

Whether you wander the paths

Or take the highway through life

It'll lead you to the end of the path

Just believe and have hope

Have hope that you'll find your way

That the earth will give you her blessing

And your rewards be plentiful

When you see land that contrasts the blue of the sea

May it fill you with joy

TYRANNY OF THE NIGHT

When darkness swallows the sky

The king of shadows takes rule over the land

The king, in his tyranny, curses all with fear

And the previously kind world is corrupted with

darkness

Pastel light glazes over you

Sleep, dreamy

But it gets interrupted

By morning dew

And cold winds

The dawn breaks around me,

And the chilling winds settle;

The cursed king's spell has released me,

When the white light drowns me, I stumble and go

The giant trees loom over me,

Their branches and shadows clawing out to me;

I hear the king's howl of rage, the darkness chases after me,

As I go, towards the piercing light

The open meadows around me, the grass swaying in the breeze

The light fills me with warmth,

Blowing away the king's darkness,

And I will go, with the light

SPRING CLEANING

Clutter, paper, books

Scattered, stacked, scuffed

Sorting, trashing, moving

Vacuumed and put away

Hidden treasures unearthed

Memories flooding back

Gentle breezes from the window

Filled with the scent of flowers and grass

The cleanliness welcoming

Only to disappear in a fortnight

LULLABY OF THE NIGHT SKY

Drowsy eyes and cloudy thoughts

The sky merely a void

The moon the center

The layers inviting sweet rest

The soft clouds beckoning

All I can do

Is give in to temptation

And drift away

To a land of rest

THE COURT'S MUSIC

The thudding of feet

The squeaking of shoes

The bouncing of balls

The shouting of people

Running down the court

Passing the ball

Breaking their ankles

The wind-up

The flick of the wrist

Swish

A TEACHER'S INFLUENCE

When I first saw you I thought nothing of you

As my teacher it was your job to teach

But as your student I did not listen

I was in my world at that time

But you knocked on my door and brought me to yours

You opened my eyes to the reality of this world

And now it is time for me to set out on my own

I came in with you as a boy

Now I set out by myself as a man

Hee hee hee

Squack!

Ahem!

I'm Awake!

Oh, Good Grief…

AAUGH!

Watch it beagle!

Psychiatric help 5 ¢

The doctor is **In**

THE MONOTONE MARCH TO GLORY

Here my journey started,

I have prepared for this my whole life

Fighting and rising to the top

To be given this chance to achieve honor!

I could imagine the trials and tests ahead of me

The challenge and glory that awaits!

Exciting and rushing my blood

Oh, the thrill!

Now 8 months later, all there is, is routine

Sleep, eat, and walk

Talk, learn, and work

Slowly but surely

Draining

The monotone of this path

More challenging than the largest wall in the world

Whispering doubts in my ear

Oh, I long for the glory that I seek!

The glory I looked for when I was a naive boy at the start of
my journey

Foolish enough to imagine what lies ahead

When all there is,

Is the monotone path of dust and dirt

Oh, when, Oh, when, shall I achieve the greatness I so desire?

THE INFINITE BEYOND THE SCREEN

Typing, typing, typing.

Click, clack, tap.

Endless tapping, a rhythmic beat,

Fingers flying across the keys, eyes glued to the glowing screens.

Caught in the web of time and tasks,

Freed when the day's labor finally unclasps,

It's time to explore the various worlds found in this machine,

The multiverse within beckons, releasing thoughts and dreams.

Ponder a word, a question, anything—

Every adventure starts from curiosity,

A question that seeks to be answered.

Soon the sound of clicking and tapping will fill the room With actor's voices, and the din of games.

Each click of the mouse takes users to another plane.

Each plane answers questions,

And each plane creates questions

As long as one's curiosity hungers for more

The possibilities remain boundless.

SHORT STORIES

Splish, splish, splish. All that can be heard are the footsteps treading on the puddles. And there he is, our protagonist, Shujinko, or Shu for short, wrapped in a black cloak and trudging along the road. He finds himself in the midst of a raided town. Looking around, Shu sees destroyed buildings, shattered boxes, and burning cars. A piece of fabric struggles through the wind catching his interest. As the fabric flutters away, he catches a glimpse of a golden triangular symbol and recognizes it right away as Oscurodis Ttrutore. Now, Oscurodis Ttrutore (or O.T. for short) is your average evil organization that wants to take over the world and be the most powerful thing on earth, only because they have nothing better to do. Now, back to the action! Live from the brain of Shu!

I glance at the symbol of O.T. taken away by the wind and run through the town streets, panting, frantically looking around, watching out for anything that could lead me to them. Broken cargo, knocked-over stands, burning cars, and shattered glass— everything seems so fresh, it couldn't have been more than an hour since O.T. came through here! Where are they? I can still smell the foul fuel mixing with the fumes of the burning town. I can't lose another lead, this one was practically given to me!

There! Something to the left! I turn and run to the corner of the block just out of sight. I can hear multiple voices yelling at each other. What is happening? "GO GO GO we're behind schedule! Take the artifacts and get into the van!" A robbery huh? No doubt it's O.T. I'm about to peek out behind the building when I'm interrupted by—"BOB! I told you to skip the concession stand while we were inside the museum! Why do you have donuts!" "But, I can't just ignore them! They were calling out to me! I swear! I had to stop and get them!" Can't blame him, I thought to myself. Man's got his priorities straight. Food first, everything else second. "They were not calling out to you! Donuts can't talk! This is ridiculous!" "Yes, they can! Donuts are all really friendly, here let me show you. This one's Harry, the chocolate one's name is Keeran, and here's Jo—" "WE DON'T HAVE TIME FOR THIS! Just get going!"

I turn the corner and around the block and I see them. The henchmen of O.T., rushing about, loading bags into a white van. Typical. I creep as close as I can to their vehicle. They haven't noticed me yet, good. They're still yelling at each other, I just need to climb onto their van without noticing. Then, vroooom, the van takes off. NO! I haven't hopped on yet. "Wait for me! Take me with youuuuu! Please don't leave without me… I may not get another chance like this." Suddenly I felt exhausted, ready to give up, like I could lie on the ground forever.

"Hey, Shu, is that you? Do you know what happened to the town? And why are you on the ground like that?" Sakura. Not *her* again, why do I have to deal with her now? Let me wallow in peace, lady. What does she want now? "Get up, you lazy bum. The ground's dirty. Is this why you left school early? To roll around in the dirt?" "Ow OW *OW!*" She's grabbing my hair! "Get. Up." "Fiiine, just stop touching my hair, it takes me an hour each morning to get it right!" It really does, I'm not exaggerating this. I really like it too, I think it makes me look like my favorite anime character, although Sakura says I don't. I just think she's jealous 'cause she could never look as good as me. But oh well.

"Haha, hey Shu I got dragged here… again." Oh, it's Roi. (His name is actually Omoshiroi, but we call him Roi.)

He observes the scene. Suddenly his eyes light up. "Oh hey, O.T. left a box of donuts on the ground. Let's see… there are three left! What a grab! These guys all deserve names. I think I'll name the first one Harry, the chocolate one Keeran, and this last one… Joey." What… how—Wha—how did he name them exactly the same as that O.T. henchman? "Hey Shu, what's with that shocked look on your face?" "Uh—It's nothing. …Why did you name them?" "Well, every registered dessert connoisseur knows that every donut deserves to be named before being eaten. It's practically a law at this point. If you forget to do so, you could be arrested by the G.B.F.I. As a junior dessert connoisseur in training, I can't forget; it would be an embarrassment and a crime." "What's the G.B.F.I.?" Sakura asks. "The Global Bureau of Food Investigation, duh," Roi and I both reply. I mean, what else could it stand for? The Genial Banding of Furry Iguanas? Roi turns to me. "The donut-naming rule only applies to the dessert branch of the organization."

Ah. That's why I didn't know about it, I'm a noodle connoisseur specializing in ramen. The different branches of the G.B.F.I. each have a set of rules. For example, in the noodle branch, you **must** start with the broth of ramen before tasting anything else. If not, you will be put on trial with a fine of up to $5000, 3 months of prison, and a suspension of your connoisseur license, if they want, the restaurant is legally allowed to sue you for disrespect as well.

Sakura wasn't getting it. "So you're saying that I could get arrested for not naming my donuts? Ridiculous, I should have been arrested over a thousand times then." "The rule only applies to dessert connoisseurs registered with the G.B.F.I., Sakura, so you're safe." "Whatever Roi, this whole G.B.F.I. thing is still ridiculous. We're getting too sidetracked. Let's track down those henchmen!" Before I could admonish Sakura for disrespecting my authority as the decision-maker, a black SUV skids to a stop right beside us and a man with a black suit and sunglasses gets out of the passenger seat.

"Mr. Shu and Mr. Roi," he says in a professional and serious tone. "Please, if you would, come with me into the car. The organization would like to talk with you both. If you must, your other companion may come as well." The organization? As in G.B.F.I.? It all made me slightly confused and nervous. (I mean, I was just confused, definitely not nervous. I'm a man, men don't get nervous. I'm sure the other two were scared for their lives, though. Also, Roi doesn't count, he's still a boy, not a man, even though I'm only older by a month.) We shuffle into the car and find another suited man waiting for us on a video call on a tablet. Oh god, what's happening now? Is it some sort of rule that we're not allowed to tell others about G.B.F.I.?

The man on the tablet speaks. "Apologies for not introducing myself and the organization. I am the general's assistant from the Global Bureau of Food Investigation, at your service. And for your information, Ms. Sakura, the G.B.F.I. is not an organization made up by some boys as a joke, but it is an internationally funded organization that Mr. Shu and Roi are both members of, as connoisseur and junior connoisseurs they are considered as "citizens" of the organization that are mostly prioritized with making sure that local restaurants serving food in a nearby connoisseur's expertise are doing so correctly and without any sacrilegious incidents." Sakura can't speak. This makes me very happy."Oh. Ok." "Ms. Sakura We are looking forward to working with you in order to put a stop to O.T.. Additionally, we have uncovered some information regarding their whereabouts. The main headquarters are located near your current location. About 60 miles north a series of warehouses is believed to be the prime suspect of their position. We will provide transportation and equipment for the three of you. You all will rendezvous with a small squad of our elite connoisseurs to assist you all, as soon as possible. Please, be safe, and good luck in your attempt to disband O.T."

With that, the tablet turns off and we are left in silence. I don't know what the other two are thinking, but now is my time to shine. I can finally take revenge on O.T. and redeem myself for my parents and Mentor-san. "Well boys,"—I include Sakura in this—she likes to be included—"I guess it really is time to finish our journey. We can finally put a stop to O.T. now."

Before they can answer, the car's doors open and we can see the bodyguard from before. "If you all would like, we can take you to pick up your equipment and immediately head to the rendezvous location." And so we go, the three of us squished into the back row of seats, and endure the long ride. I fully expect there to be a bunch of top-secret technology inside the car, so I spend an hour fidgeting… It turns out it's a regular car. I'm a bit disappointed by this. I think Roi is, too.

Eventually, the road changes from pavement to dirt and gravel and the car stops. I'm confused. There are no signs of the enemy headquarters; all I can see is the dirt trail and the forest around us. "Alright, please prepare for the mission. I will hand out the equipment from the trunk. Please come out when you three are ready," says our suit guy. Finally! I've been waiting my whole life for this! Our battle will be legendary! Ack! I don't even mind that my legs are almost numb from that never-ending car ride. What kind of gear am I gonna get to defeat my arch-nemesis? Maybe some laser guns or a grappling hook! The man continues, "I have been provided a set of combat gear for each of you. It should help you but be mindful of the slightly hazardous items. You have not been given any weapon that could be severely dangerous on account that you have not received any training. Good luck, and do your best."

"Thank you, sir!" all three of us say. I wonder what he's gonna give us!! The representative takes out three sleek, jet-black briefcases and hands them out to us. I take a moment to admire the fancy-looking case. I can't wait to open it and find out what my epic avenging weapon of justice will be!

I undo the clasps and swiftly open it up. Inside I can see a bulletproof vest, gloves, walkie-talkies, and—oh look! A taser! Fun! And for the weapon of justice…Weird. Nothing else in the box. With the normal car and the non-epic gear, I'm a little disappointed in G.B.F.I. The representative calls us to focus. "You may be wondering about the desolate surroundings. I have stopped us here so that we are not detected by O.T., as there is a checkpoint guarding their base. You must bypass without setting off the alarms. One of our elite forces is coming to help you, so please, do not worry about backup." "Let's go guys we gotta stop O.T. as soon as we can!" "Sakura you gotta let us gear up first!" Roi replies to her. Well, this is it… the finale to my life's mission. I wonder what'll happen after this.

The three of us are lying low in the undergrowth right now. The checkpoint is about 5 feet in front of us. I can see 2 guards, one inside the little shack, and the other outside, chatting with the first. Being the absolute genius that I am, I recall one of the most sacred stealth techniques Mentor-san taught me, and I throw a stone across the road from us to distract the guards.

It looks like the first guard outside the toll booth has taken notice of the movement. He cautiously approaches with his fellow henchmen, and when they bend over to inspect, that's when we strike. Like a pair of cheetahs, Sakura and I dash across the road and taze them before they realize it. We handcuff the two and then we slink back into the forest, trudging toward their headquarters.

"… And there I was, completely hidden beneath the shrubs and grasses, planning my next move, waiting for the perfect chance to sneak through the gate unnoticed." "Ugh, Shu, why are you monologuing again? You're not an anime or book

character, you know. Are you forgetting that we're here too?" "Yeah Shu, Sakura, and I wanna be part of the story too, you know?" They just don't understand. Well, Roi sort of does, but he's got a long way to go. "You guys! In order to be a cool protagonist, you have to monologue at least once before a super-important event happens. I practice my monologuing every morning before I leave for school." "Really? Alright then, how should we start a monologue?" "You have to start it with the deepest voice you can make, then make everything sound dark and serious." **"It was dark outside, searchlights rushing past us searching in vain—"**

Oh god, that's not Sakura's voice… we're surrounded by O.T. henchmen, and the G.B.F.I. symbol is on our vests in full view! The voice continues. "As much as I would like to take monologuing lessons from you myself, you're part of the G.B.F.I., so unfortunately, I have to take you three to the boss and let him do his thing. Tie them up, boys." I won't let this happen! It's time to pull out the hero card. "Wait! I'll give all of you free monologuing lessons for one month if you don't tie us up! I'll give you guys the premium package including the exclusive voice-deepening exercise only I know!" "Tempting. Get going, boy." Unbelievable. The hero card has never failed before! We're forced to walk through the gates and into the main building. We're blasted with AC upon entering and the floors are covered in white marble. The men lead us up to the top floor where they leave us in front of a pair of large heavy doors. Wait. They're… leaving us?

I'm so nervous—uh, I mean, confused—that I temporarily give up my decision-making role. "Uhh… any ideas, guys? What do we do now—" And the doors open. "Ahh, welcome in! It's so good to finally meet you." So this is it.

I step forward into a brightly lit room. Once my eyes adjust to the blinding lights, I see him—or his back. He's turning around in his chair like an utter creep. Only missing a cat. *Come on. Let me see your face.*

At last, my arch-nemesis comes to a full stop, clasps his hands, and— "Wait, why do you kind of look like Shu?" Roi points out, and he's right? He does look like me! "Of course I do, Shu might not know why, but there's no reason for him not to look like me." I am so confused right now, why is saying that as if he's related to me? I'm an adopted child who has no memory of his own parents!

"It may be surprising news to you all, but I am Shu's father." "What?!" What? He's my father? I mean he looks like he could be, but I don't even have any memories of him! "Thirteen years ago, I left to go buy milk from the supermarket with my wife and had just ordered pineapple pizza. Unfortunately, I didn't know that the G.B.F.I had banned pineapple on pizza, so the pizzeria raised the alarm and I was ambushed by the organization. We were forced to leave Shu behind at home, so we contacted Mentor San to take care of him. Ever since then, we have formed Oscurodis Ttrutore to fight back! Join me Shu, and we can liberate the world of the organization and legalize pineapple on pizza!"

"These are my parents? Criminals against the organization? I can't believe it! Unacceptable! I could never join you! Even if you weren't criminals, I can't really view you as my parents, I barely even know who you are, and It's been my whole life goal to take O.T. down! I think it's time to put an end to this atrocity!" *Click*

The ceiling of the building explodes, and agents of the GBFI descend from the sky. And my 'Father' looks at me with sad eyes, "I see, then I have no reason to fight back. I'm sorry I failed you. I guess you're loyalty as a dog to the organization is more important to you than your kin."

The agents arrest him and take him away in helicopters and that's it. "Wow, we really did it," says Roi. It's a bit of an underwhelming end to my lifetime goal but I've done it. We've destroyed O.T. and arrested the leader behind it. I wonder what comes next? Maybe I'll travel the world and expand my knowledge of food. It might be fun to aim to be the best connoisseur in the world, but for now, I'll just enjoy my win. It's time to head home and celebrate with pizza.

HOW THE CHRYSANTHEMUMS CAME TO HAVE THEIR COLORS

When the world was still young and full of life, during the time of Gods, Heroes, and Monsters, stood the city of Dexsibe, a beacon of life in the sandy deserts of Mesopotamia. The Dexsibe people were exiles from Egypt due to their devotion to Gaia, the goddess of life. Gaia blessed Dexsibe with an oasis that supplied the exiles with dates, wheat, rich soil, and freshwater. With time, Dexsibe became a city known for being the pinnacle of life.

As Dexsibe's prosperity, popularity, and population grew, so did the dangers it faced. Monsters, demons, and neighboring cities threatened the peace of Dexsibe, and the citizens decided that it was time for Dexsibe to once again choose a Champion.

Champions were warriors sworn to protect their towns and people. According to Dexsibian tradition, candidates were voted in by their fellow citizens, and a series of tests determined whether they met the prerequisites: extraordinary strength, speed, and intelligence. Once Champions were chosen, they were revered in their city and had an almost King-like status until the end of their days. The Champion of Dexsibe at the time of our story is Akshaz, whose ability to overpower a bear and out-trick a sphinx had made him the top choice for Champion in the eyes of the people.

Our story starts with Akshaz's return from a battle with a monstrous boar in a neighboring city. He marched triumphantly to his home – only to discover his beloved town of Dexsibe under a plague. Alu, the demon of sickness and pestilence, in an effort to avenge his humiliation and defeat at the hands of Akshaz in a previous battle, had sprinkled his pestilence potion into the heart of the city's oasis. The demon chuckled in glee as he witnessed from a distance the disease spreading through the city like wildfire. As citizens continued to use the water for their everyday needs, more and more people caught the disease, leaving them unable to move, their bodies burning up from fever, with black patches covering their skin. When Champion Akshaz arrived, he feared it may have been too late.

As the plague engulfed the city, panicked citizens began looting and rioting, believing the end times had arrived. Some set up barriers around certain areas in desperate attempts to contain the spread. In response, the city council called an emergency gathering of the wisest men in Dexsibe at the city's fabled oasis. An elderly man approached the podium in the center of the theater, surrounded by primarily unfilled seats. Paciriac, the oldest and wisest council member, addressed the men in attendance wearing his signature two-piece purple tunic and the most meager of sandals.

"My friends and fellow citizens of Dexsibe. We are gathered here to address the sickness that oppresses our city. As some of you may know, we have been visited by a demon who has cursed our city's oasis. The doctors, herbalists, and priests have done their best to lift this affliction on us, but alas, it's to no avail! Our only hope now is to seek the mythical flower of Gula, capable of healing anyone of any illness or disability that may impede a person. According to legend, the magical plant is located in the Atlas Mountains. It's our priority to find the flower before we are forced to flee the land our goddess Gaia has given us. It is in our best interest to send our Champion Akshaz, to set out on this quest and retrieve Gula's flower."

The council members whispered among themselves in discussion as Paciriac closed his speech and shuffled back to his front-row seat, holding his signature rugged cane, which stood a foot taller than himself.

The council then rose unanimously and declared in perfect unison: "Our Champion Ashkaz will be dispatched to find the flower."

The next day, as the burning sun peeked over the mountains, Akshaz and his mother rose from their beds and ate Akshaz's favorite meal together, heavenly homemade lamb stew, as they always did before the hero left for a quest. The pair then began their walk, hand-in-hand, to the temple of the gods. The temple, built of glistening white marble and twenty feet tall with statues of the gods, was cool to the touch when the duo entered. They prayed, offering Gaea and Gula the lamb stew from the morning. Akshaz's mother talked to the goddesses, entreating them to ensure that her son would come home safely. When she left, Akshaz was alone. He stood, ready to receive guidance.

No one knows what goes on in the temple when a Champion is alone; all that is known is that Champions leave with more confidence, wisdom, and strength.

As Akshaz emerged from the shrine, he walked to his prepared chariot where a trusted servant gave him his shining suit of armor to put on. Out of the corner of Akshaz's eyes, he could see his adventure basket containing candied fruits, loaves of bread, and a couple of wedges of goat cheese. Akshaz looked forward to the meals with his adventure basket, and in high spirits, he gripped the reins of his chariot and rode through the city. To his surprise, the people of Dexsibe had gathered despite the sickness to see their Champion off. Akshaz waved at the crowds, and they roared back in hopes that their Champion would find the flower of Gula before the city fell into chaos.

Akshaz gazed through the wind while the clouds zipped past the carriage and Carthage, a large and prosperous city known for impressive harbors and ports, slowly came into view. As the city closest to the Atlassian Mountain Range, it would provide a much-needed resting point and an opportunity to learn the quickest path to his destination. Akshaz descended into the city and guided his chariot to the flaming inn. The dark, gritty atmosphere would be perfect for ordering a drink, getting comfortable, and starting a conversation.

"Wouldst thou like a drink and hot meal?" Asked the owner of the establishment as he walked up to the counter.

Akshaz responded with a light nod. As the food was prepared, the chatty owner wasted no time making conversation.

"It's a den for traveling and visitors today. It must be. Another one, just like thee, was in hither earlier going on about a flower with the ability to heal, if thou can believe it." Immediately, Akshaz remembered a feeling he had earlier—a feeling that he would not be the only one seeking the flower.

"What did this man look like?" He asked the innkeeper as his meal was placed in front of him.

"Full of himself, that one is. Walks around with a kaunake longer than a flowing river and a sword adorned with precious stones."

Akshaz immediately knew of whom the owner spoke. It was Molot of Gibraltar, a skilled champion with whom Akshaz once slayed a dragon. Molot was known for his affinity for the cloth of kaunake. He also had a turbulent history with the demon known as Alu. It was believed that the region Molot hailed from had recently suffered a similar fate as Dexsibe. It all suddenly made sense to Akshaz. Molot was after the flower for the same reason: to save his people.

The innkeeper continued, "Aye, that flower. It's said to bloom only once every hundred years. Supposed to sit in a flourishing valley full of magic between the mountain peaks, a singular rainbow flower that grows independently. That other fellow believes the next one will bloom in half a week."

Akshaz knew that his window of time had just shrunk considerably; he was nearly a five-day journey from the mountain's peak, and Molot was also after the flower. With no time to waste, Akshaz finished his meal and immediately headed out through an isolated road the innkeeper informed him of that led directly to the summit.

After a day's journey, Akshaz stopped to rest and eat. After cooking a hot meal, he set up camp and accidentally dozed off.

After what felt like a fortnight, he was awakened by a deep, rumbling growl. Akshaz opened his eyes to see a gaze piercing through him in the dark. He silently rose from the ground and got into his fighting stance. A second later, a blur jumped out of the undergrowth and tackled Akshaz, but he drew his sword and blocked his opponent. He then spotted his foe, a majestic leopard with two mighty wings on its back, called a lamassus. Both the beast and hero charged at each other, exchanging blows and dodging them. The monster stepped back, reared up, and flapped his mighty wings. Akshaz was blown straight into a tree with a loud THUD, and the lamassus took its chance to deal the finishing blow. The winged beast lifted its claws and opened its jaws, when SHUNK—its head fell off its body in a rainbow and silver blur. Dead.

"Stay down, evil monster! I, Molot, command you."

And here our hero found Molot, with his jewel-studded sword out and covered in blood.

As Akshaz recovered from his light wounds, he thanked his fellow champion. "Greetings, Champion Molot. What brings you here?"

Molot replied, "I heard that you, too, are after the flower of Gula to heal your city of disease? If so, I would like to propose traveling to the Mountains of Atlas together, for my city too is suffering from an incurable disease. Traveling together will ensure that we reach the mountains safely."

Knowing it was in his best interest to comply, Akshaz agreed to Molot's plans, and the two champions began their journey to the Atlas mountains together.

Determined to retrieve the magical flower, they used their immense strength to sprint through the mountains and the trees. Throughout the day, they split up; Akshaz looked for the valley adorned with plants, while Molot searched aimlessly, not having the same knowledge Akshaz had from the innkeeper. He saw Molot speeding through the forest faster than a young leopard, frantically looking for signs that could lead him to the healing flower.

Akshaz continued to scan the landscape and, in the corner of his eye, saw a faint glint in the distance, no doubt caused by magic. Akshaz's heart sped up, unable to contain the excitement and joy of possibly finding the cure to his city's deadly disease.

Hearing the sound of Akshaz's running, Molot, curious about where Akshaz was going, headed in his direction. As soon as Molot looked beyond his fellow champion, he saw the shining light in the distance. Both warriors were now confident that the light they saw in the rising dark of the evening was where the flower they sought was located.

It was just before dawn when Akshaz reached the top of the valley. The valley was bathed in light as if the sun was at its highest point, blessing the earth with its warmth. Vibrant green grasses coated the valley, waving in the slight breeze. A crystal clear river babbled through the seemingly magical place, and flowers, flowers of all types, dotted the valley—blood red roses without thorns, lilies displaying ornate patterns, and daisies of the purest white and golden pistils. Enchanted by the beauty of the plain, Akshaz walked towards the valley's center, careful not to step on any flowers. As the champion walked toward the valley's center, he saw the object of his quest—a flower, glowing with magic, growing on an ornate stone pedestal.

The flower's beauty rivaled that of the gods: its petals were as numerous as the grains of sand on the earth, each petal a different vibrant color as if the flower was a rainbow. Captured by its beauty, Akshaz reached out to pick the flower—and he heard a large thud behind him.

He whipped around to see who interrupted him, hoping it would be Molot, but to his horror, it was Alu, the demon of sickness and pestilence, along with his companion, Basmu, the winged serpent.

Akshaz cried out to the monsters, "What business do you have here?"

Alu responded, "Hand over the flower of Gula, and there will be peace throughout the land.

Unknown to the monster duo, Molot had arrived at the valley. Scanning the area, he spotted the magical flower on its pedestal and could sense the magical barrier protecting it. Near the flower, he saw Akshaz and Basmu negotiating for the flower, and crept down the valley. Just as the demon sensed Molot's presence, Molot swooped in, delivering a kick to the demon's stomach and sending him flying into the barrier.

The barrier, only allowing humans and gods to enter inside, instantly disintegrated Alu, leaving only a trail of dust, sending the foul monster to the underworld, as he screamed in agony. Both Basmu and Akshaz stood, gawking, staring at the ashes of the demon. Enraged at his comrade's death, Basmu let out a ground-shaking roar, and Molot and Akshaz prepared to fight the massive serpent.

The champions rushed at the monster. The serpent spread his wings and lashed out with his tail. Molot met it head-on with all his strength, nullifying the blow, as Akshaz leapt toward the head of the beast, poised to bash its skull. Basmu attempted to shield the blow with his mighty wings but was hit with the might of Akshaz. The serpent wrestled with the two champions, trying to squeeze Molot with his body and push Akshaz away from his head. The champions knew that the weakness of all serpents is in their heads.

Suddenly, Molot gave a mighty cry and punched through Basmu's thick scales. The monster screeched in pain as Molot continued to rip the scales off of the serpent. Basmu reeled back and briefly forgot about Akshaz, who took his chance and jumped as high as he could, coming down on the serpent's wings and head with a mighty kick. Akshaz's heel smashed through Basmu's wings and met the monster's skull. The snake thrashed in pain and was met with another thunderous blow from Molot under his jaw, and Basmu's skull shattered instantly, killing the beast and splattering its remains throughout the valley.

Exhausted, the two heroes stood, covered in sweat.

As they recovered, a hissing sound was heard near the flower. The champions whipped around, and the flower split into numerous flowers that began to cover the valley, each a single color, unlike before.

The champions were amazed at the miracle they were witnessing and were even more shocked when they heard the voice of the goddess Gula herself: "O heroes of the earth, thank you for driving off the monsters. Without you, they would have set free all the monsters of the Underworld and taken revenge on everyone on this planet. My flower has split, so you can both cure your people."

The goddess left. Akshaz and Molot picked as many flowers as they could, feeling the blossoms' power surge through them, and rushed into the horizon, back to their cities, to cure them of their plagues. Molot and Akshaz descended the Atlassian Mountains and hurried home, each going their separate ways.

When he arrived, Akshaz was greeted by the sight and smell of sickness throughout the city. The hero, in panic at the sight of so many people sick and dying, grabbed his bag of magical flowers and ran to the herbalists. They almost fainted at the sight of so many flowers that had the potential to heal a single person's sickness. To heal the city's entire population, the herbalists worked as they had never worked before, extracting the essence of magic from the leaves and mixing it into the oasis. As the flowers worked their magic into the contaminated oasis, the pervasive sickness could be felt leaving the city. The people who were ill could now heal themselves from the plague if they simply drank from the now-magical oasis. Crowds came to the oasis to cure themselves of the plague. All was going well for the city; the people were happy, and the disease was being healed.

But happiness can't last forever.

A messenger sprinted toward Akshaz, panting hard, as he brought mortifying news to the champion that his mother was dying of the plague and that the now healing water of the oasis was useless for people at death's doors. The devastating news hit Akshaz hard. He sprinted to his dying mother.

When she caught sight of him entering her bedroom, she smiled at him and managed to whisper, "I am proud of your good work, and please, do not be ashamed that you could not save me."

She took her last breath.

Enraged, Akshaz howled and screamed in grief. His tears and howling were so powerful that every magical flower in the city of Dexsibe was stained with a second color: dark blue, blood red, blazing orange, and many other intense colors changed the flowers forever. In grief for his beloved mother, he called these flowers "Chrysanthemums" in honor of her.

And that is the story of the great Akshaz of Dexsibe, and how chrysanthemums came to have different colors.

THE GREATEST CHANGE OF THE CENTRAL REGISTRY, IN THE PERSPECTIVE OF SAMUEL SOBOLEV, A CLERK OF THE REGISTRY

In an unnamed city, in an unnamed country, is a great building with the words, "The Central Registry of Births, Marriages, and Death" above the doorway engraved in black on a white plaque. The building, resembling a library, is outdated, and the paint and enamel on the walls have been whittled away by age, cracking, peeling, and chipping. This dreary building is where I work. As I, Samuel Sobolev, a proud clerk of the Central Registry, enter the building, I am greeted by the thick smell of aged paper and musty ink. The Registry contains a group of fifteen personnel, working to maintain an accurate archive of the significant changes in the lives of the people in our community. It is an honor for me to be part of the Central Registry and serve the people. The only drawback to the work we do is that everything must be handwritten on paper cards as per tradition, hence the smell of old paper. Every weekday I work at the registry, as it is closed on the weekends. I create and update the cards of the living and move the occasional card from the half of the registry containing the information of the living to the other half containing the information of the dead.

It's been two years since I joined the ranks of the Central Registry, and it has been a great time so far, despite the strict regulations on appearances and the considerable amount of work I am given. Although I suppose it is because of all the potential they see in me to improve the registry's operations, that they give me all of this work. I do have to say though, the pay I receive has blown me out of the water! It is so much more than what I expected from working in this old crusty building. But as a service of the government, I suppose the Central Registry has sufficient funding to compensate us this well.

Today I headed to my usual work desk twenty minutes before we opened to the public, and set my briefcase down. I then walked over to the desks of the senior clerk in charge of managing me and another clerk, to receive the lists of tasks that I should complete before we close today at eight o'clock. It is quite a lengthy list, but not quite the longest I have seen before, and I am certain that I will be able to complete my tasks before closing time. After analyzing my agenda and making sure I had no questions to ask, I returned to my desk, pulling out the pen and inkwell the registrar gave me.

Just as the registry opens, he comes in. No, not the Registrar, but another clerk, Senhor Jose, was running late and rushing in instead of the Registrar. Senhor Jose has recently been getting into a lot of action, being called to the Registrar's desk, almost running late on multiple occasions, and leaving an hour earlier than everyone else! I believe that Senhor Jose has to get back into his right state of mind before he makes too big of a mistake. Just because he has been working at the Central Registry for almost twenty years and is most likely the Registrar's favorite employee, doesn't mean that he can change his attitude towards the Registry and its staff. I mean, look at him right now! He's all out of place, with an unshaven beard, messy hair, and an unironed uniform. His tie isn't even worn correctly! As he approaches his senior clerk, late and tripping over his shoelaces, he tells him the reason why he was late for the day. I look around to see the reactions of my fellow clerks, senior clerks, and deputies and I see some of them with smug looks on their faces and others with disappointed looks.

At this point Senhor Jose is doomed, he's either going to be reprimanded by the Registrar or be fired altogether from the

Central Registry if he walks into the building any time now… Or not? It's now been five minutes and we are all standing at our desks waiting for the registrar to arrive and start our day off. We're all nervous right now, the Registrar is usually at least ten minutes early. We waited for what seemed like an eternity, there was no message from the Registrar yesterday or previously telling us that he wouldn't be here, and no one had come by to tell us that he was sick and was unable to come to the Central Registry.

It has been an hour after our usual opening time, and at this point, I am starting to sweat, the deputies are about to fill in for the Registrar himself and start the day, but then I see him, coming through the doors of the building in such a dignified and reserved manner, that everyone immediately goes back to standing next their desks and anxiously waiting for anything he has to say. At first, I thought that he had woken up late or had a bad sleep, but as I kept my gaze on him, I realized that this was not the case, because, unlike Senhor Jose, his appearance is composed, with his hair combed, suit perfectly ironed out, face flawlessly shaved, and tie on right. He starts walking to his desk in the back of the registry but slows when he reaches Senhor Jose's desk. I can see Senhor Jose raising his arm halfway, probably to scratch his chin, but puts it back down midway, then the Registrar continues to his desk, calling his two deputies to come with him.

Now, Senhor Jose is done for, the Registrar most likely wants his deputies' input about him and will fire the man because of his change in attitude to the Registry. As the deputies and registrar finish talking, one walks toward the front doors and puts up a sign telling the public that we are temporarily closed, and the other turns towards the rest of us and declares "Attention clerks and senior clerks, the Registrar would like to have a word with all of us". We all turned our chairs around to face him and silence followed. Clearing his voice, the Registrar talks about how we still use inkwells and blotters to maintain tradition, and that tradition is what keeps the Central Registry alive. He continues talking surprisingly about the changes to the registry that were brought up, bringing up the incident where the deputy suggested the reordering of the archives, and when a genealogist lost himself in the building, barely alive. The Registrar then hits us with the largest task ever assigned to any of us. He proposes the reorganization of the cards of the people, sorting from the most recent lives to the earliest ones.

I can see jaws dropping at the mention of this impossible plan, but at least he doesn't expect us to finish it, as he knows it will take decades to even make noticeable progress in the rearrangement of the archives. Other than the changes to the archives themselves, the protocols and rules of the Central Registry will remain the same, with strict dress codes and personal behavior during work. The Registrar trails off with his speech and advances toward Senhor Jose as I do my best to process everything that he just said. After a brief interaction with each other, the Registrar walks away from Senhor Jose's desk and I guess we go straight to work???

This has been a confusing, frightening, and surprisingly eventful day for the Registry so far. It is now our job at the Central Registry to reorder ALL of the cards so that the people who are living in the present are closest to the front of the Registry and those who lived during the time of the opening of the Registry, the furthest away, and integrate the living and the dead cards together? Absolutely ridiculous, though I suppose that now, everyone, including the Registrar himself will have to contribute to restructuring the gargantuan archives. While I pondered about how the reorganization would affect the efficiency and routine of the Central Registry, the deputy took down the sign and officially opened the registry for the day, and

I got started on the now grueling list of tasks I needed to complete by today, as the Registrar, Deputies, and Senior Clerks all gathered together to plan the reconstitution of the archives.

*This short story draws inspiration from a scene in José Saramago's acclaimed novel All the Names, a creative masterpiece that follows the journey of Senhor José, the Central Registry, and the file card of an ordinary woman.

AUTHOR

Yale Ryan Kwon, a dedicated student at Thomas Jefferson High School for Science and Technology, has been passionate about storytelling since a young age. As the founder of the Youth Alliance for Limitless Engagement (Y.A.L.E.) Foundation, a non-profit organization, Yale actively contributes his musical and artistic talents to his local community. Despite the challenges of high school life, he crafts imaginative narratives that captivate readers. Beyond writing, Yale enjoys reading, volleyball, video games, and spending time with friends. His creative works are a testament to his diverse interests, promising a bright future in the literary world.

www.ingramcontent.com/pod-product-compliance
Lightning Source LLC
Chambersburg PA
CBHW061552310726
48972CB00008B/2726